NORWOOD HOUSE PRESS

Alphabet Authors

By Kathleen Corrigan

Search for Sounds
Vowels: a, i

T0062100

Scan this code to access the Teacher's Notes for this series or visit
www.norwoodhousepress.com/decodables

DEAR CAREGIVER, *The Decodables* series contains books following a systematic, cumulative phonics scope and sequence aligned with the science of reading. Each book in the *Search for Sounds* series allows its reader to apply their phonemic awareness and phonics knowledge in engaging and relatable texts. The keywords within each text have been carefully selected to allow readers to identify pictures beginning with sounds and letters they have been explicitly taught.

When reading these books with your child, encourage them to isolate the beginning sound in the keywords, find the corresponding picture, and identify the letter that makes the beginning sound by pointing to the letter placed in the corner of each page. Rereading the texts multiple times will allow your child the opportunity to build their letter sound fluency, a skill necessary for decoding.

You can be confident you are providing your child with opportunities to build their foundational decoding abilities which will encourage their independence as they become lifelong readers.

Happy Reading!

Emily Nudds, M.S. Ed Literacy
Literacy Consultant

C

D

5

6

C

D

A

B

i

8

C

D

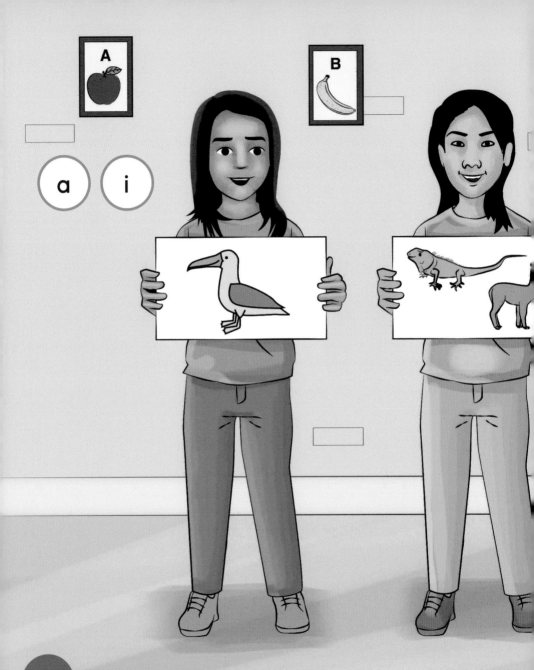

C

D

HOW TO USE THIS BOOK

Read this text with your child as they engage with each page. Then, read each keyword and ask them to isolate the beginning sound before finding the corresponding picture in the illustration. Encourage finding and pointing to the corresponding letter in the corner of the page. Additional reinforcement activities can be found in the Teacher's Notes.

Alphabet Authors
a

Pages 2 and 3	Hi! I am Zara and I am in kindergarten. We are making alphabet books in our class. Our big reading buddies are helping us write our stories. My reading buddy is Alice. She is in fifth grade, so she can write a lot of words. Our story is about an alligator!
	One day the alligator went for a walk on the avenue beside his river. He saw some books in the grass beside the avenue. One book was an atlas. An atlas is a book full of maps. The alligator looked at the maps. Another book was an alphabet book. The alligator looked at the alphabet book. He saw food in the book.
	The alligator said, "I am hungry. Where is an animal for me to eat?" But all the animals, like rabbits, raccoons, and a cat, were running to hide from the alligator. He kept walking on the avenue.

Keywords: Alice, alligator, alphabet, atlas, avenue, cat, maps

Pages 4 and 5	Soon the alligator came to a garden. Abby was picking asters in her garden. When she saw the alligator, Abby ran to her apple tree and climbed up. An apple fell on the alligator's head. He was angry. Then he looked at the apples on the ground and began to eat them. Soon he had a tummy full of apples and he fell asleep.

Abby looked at the alligator. He snored. Abby crept down from the apple tree and ran quickly to her house. She didn't want to meet an alligator with a tummy ache! |

Keywords: Abby, alligator, apple, asters, axe

Read this text with your child as they engage with each page. Then, read each keyword and ask them to isolate the beginning sound before finding the corresponding picture in the illustration. Encourage finding and pointing to the corresponding letter in the corner of the page. Additional reinforcement activities can be found in the Teacher's Notes.

i

Pages 6 and 7	Hi! I am Victor and I am in kindergarten, too. My reading buddy is Isabel. She can write a lot of words. Our story is about an impala and an iguana.
	One day an impala was eating grass in a field. An iguana climbed up the impala and put itchy powder on his back. The iguana thought it was funny but it was mean. The impala jumped and rolled and ran. He rubbed his back on a tree. But his back was too itchy!
	Then the impala rolled in a puddle of ink. He rolled and rolled until the itch stopped.

Keywords: iguana, impala, inchworm, ink, insect, Isabel, itchy

i

Pages 8 and 9
The impala marched over to the iguana. He put his nose one inch from the iguana. He said, "That was mean."

The iguana said, "It was a joke. It was funny."

The impala said, "It was not funny. You should go far, far away. I don't want to see you anymore. You are not my friend."

The iguana was surprised. She did not want to be mean. She left the impala and all their friends. She went far, far away so she could think and think and not be mean. It got cold and dark, so the iguana crawled into an igloo and stayed there until spring.

Then she went back to the impala and said, "I am sorry. Itchy powder is not fun. Can we be friends?" And they were friends again.

Keywords: igloo, iguana, impala, insect

a, i

Pages 10 and 11
We wrote funny stories. They have lots of animals in them. We will make some *a* and *i* animal pages for our alphabet book. Let's list the animals we thought of: an albatross bird, alligator, alpaca, iguana, inchworm, insect, and impala.

Can you think of more?

Keywords: albatross, Alice, alligator, alpaca, alphabet, iguana, impala, inchworm, insect, Isabel

Norwood House Press • www.norwoodhousepress.com
The Decodables ©2024 by Norwood House Press. All Rights Reserved.
Printed in the United States of America.
367N—082023

Library of Congress Cataloging-in-Publication Data has been filed and is available at
https://lccn.loc.gov/2023024995

Literacy Consultant: Emily Nudds, M.S.Ed Literacy
Editorial and Production Development and Management: Focus Strategic Communications Inc.
Editors: Christine Gaba, Christi Davis-Martell
Illustration Credit: Mindmax
Covers: Shutterstock, Macrovector

Hardcover ISBN: 978-1-68450-721-4   Paperback ISBN: 978-1-68404-865-6
eBook ISBN: 978-1-68404-924-0